# When the Buddha Was an Elephant

# When the Buddha Was an Elephant

## 32 ANIMAL WISDOM TALES FROM THE *JATAKA*

Written and illustrated by
## Mark W. McGinnis

Shambhala
*Boston & London*
2015

Shambhala Publications, Inc.
Horticultural Hall
300 Massachusetts Avenue
Boston, Massachusetts 02115
www.shambhala.com

9   8   7   6   5   4   3   2   1

First Edition
Printed in China

♾ This edition is printed on acid-free paper that meets the
American National Standards Institute Z39.48 Standard.
♻ Shambhala Publications makes every effort to print on recycled paper.
For more information please visit www.shambhala.com.

Distributed in the United States by Penguin Random House LLC
and in Canada by Random House of Canada Ltd

Designed by James D. Skatges

Library of Congress Cataloging-in-Publication Data

McGinnis, Mark W., 1950- author.
When the Buddha was an elephant : 32 animal wisdom tales
from the Jataka / Mark W. McGinnis.
pages   cm
Includes bibliographical references and index.
ISBN 978-1-61180-264-1 (hardback : alk. paper)
1. Tipitaka. Suttapitaka. Khuddakanikaya. Jataka—
Paraphrases, English.  2. Jataka stories, English.
3. Fables.  I. Title.
BQ1462.E5M46 2015
294.3'82325—dc23
2014048118

*Dedicated to my grandson*
*Samuel Atticus Cutler*

# Contents

# Introduction

In 2000 I went to India to travel some of the Buddhist pilgrimage paths and do research for my first book, *Buddhist Animal Wisdom Stories*. In Bodh Gaya, where the Buddha famously awakened, I found at the Mahabodhi Temple bookstore a six-volume collection of the Jataka tales, *The Jataka*, edited by E. B. Cowell and published from 1895 to 1907. This monumental work of 550 stories contains the Buddha's accounts of his incarnations in human and animal form prior to his enlightenment. From this scriptural source I gleaned the foundation for my own first volume of stories.

Fifteen years later I have returned to the Jataka for this new book. In my now tattered copies of Cowell's collection I found the inspiration for new stories. The Jataka is part of an enormous body of works belonging to the Buddhist Pali Canon. It originally provided moral tales to be taught to child monks at Buddhist monasteries, instructing them how to function in their communities and families. As with the original Jataka tales, the stories herein develop moral themes, such as following the guidance of elders, exercising wise leadership, and being truthful. Death is not avoided in the stories and is sometimes the outcome of poor decisions. Some of the stories may seem severe, but surely they pale when compared to today's popular entertainment or the nightly news.

My journey as an artist has taken me down many roads, few as satisfying as the one that led to this work and its predecessor. The problems presented to me with this kind of book—painting drawn from literature—engaged all my abilities, and solving these problems was a joy.

I hope that child and adult alike will enjoy this book and share it with others.

—Mark W. McGinnis

# The Elephant and Her Mother

 **L** **ONG AGO,** deep in the forest north of Varanasi, there lived a great, beautiful elephant who had left the herd she was leading so she could care for her blind mother. She would bring her mother fruits and leaves, and the aged elephant was deeply grateful for her daughter's loving care.

One day while the daughter was searching for food, she heard deep, mournful sobbing and looked for its source. She found a lost forester crying. Seeing the massive elephant walking toward him, the man shook with fear and ran.

"Don't be afraid," the elephant called after him. "Can I help you?"

The man stopped and said, "Oh kind one, I have been lost for days and I am starving and cannot find my way home."

The elephant picked him up, put him on her back, and took him to a fruit tree. She let him eat his fill and then brought him to a well-known road where he could easily find his way.

On his return home the man began thinking how magnificent the elephant was in both body and kindness. But he was a greedy fellow, and instead of feeling gratitude for the elephant's compassion, he began plotting in his mind. The man thought, "The king's favorite elephant has recently died, and this elephant is far greater. If I were to bring his men to capture this one, I would be richly rewarded."

So he took the news of the great elephant to the king of Varanasi, who was delighted to hear of such a creature. The king generously rewarded the forester and sent him and his most experienced men to capture the elephant. They found her drinking at a lake dappled with lotuses. The men surrounded the elephant and set their snares to capture her. The elephant was aware of the men and knew she

1

could kill them all if she wished, but it was not in her nature. She allowed herself to be captured, and when she saw the forester, who had been hiding in the brush, she thought, "So, this is how you repay my kindness."

The elephant's mother became deeply concerned when her daughter did not return, fearing that something had happened to her. She lamented, "Oh, my dear daughter, the trees will still grow and the flowers may bloom around me, but now it is truly dark without you."

The elephant was brought to the royal stables and washed and adorned. The king was delighted with the great beast and supplied her with the finest foods. But she would not eat.

Hearing of this, the king went to the elephant and said, "Dear Great One, why won't you eat? I will feed you and treat you as if you were royalty yourself. Please eat."

The elephant replied, "My blind mother is now starving in the forest because I am not there to bring food for her. I too will starve, even with these delicacies before me. I can take no food while she has none."

The king was a good man and was touched by the elephant's devotion to her mother. "You are free, my friend," he said. "My men will return you to the forest and you may go care for your beloved mother."

Alone once more beside the lake of lotuses, the elephant quickly filled her trunk with water and hurried to her weak, blind mother. The loyal daughter sprayed the water in the air, giving her mother a cool shower.

The aged elephant said to herself, "Why is it raining during this dry season? Only my daughter would bring such refreshing mist."

"It *is* me!" cried her daughter, and they entwined their trunks in a loving embrace. The great elephant brought fruit for her mother and told her of all that had occurred.

"That good king!" said the mother. "May he live long and his kingdom prosper."

# The Boar and
# the Tiger

**L**ONG AGO, south of Gaya, a village carpenter found a baby boar trapped in a pit in the forest. He took the little piglet home and raised him as a pet. The piglet grew into a very large, intelligent boar with impressive, sharp, curved tusks. With his tusks the boar would help the carpenter turn logs, and with his teeth he would chisel the wood. He was a very useful and friendly creature but also quite strong, and in time the carpenter grew concerned that the other villagers would fear the boar and kill him. So though he loved the boar very much, one day he led him deep into the forest and let him go free.

The boar wandered for many days looking for a good place to live. At last he found a wonderful cave surrounded by bulbs, roots, and fruits to eat. There he was approached by a large pack of fellow boars.

"I am glad to see you," said the carpenter's boar. "May I live in this place with you?"

"It is a nice place," said the leader of the pack, "but very dangerous. Every morning a tiger comes here and carries off any game he can find."

"Every morning?"

"Every morning."

"Only one tiger, and all of you with such large tusks?"

"Yes."

"We will put an end to this," said the carpenter's boar.

Early the next morning, before dawn, he organized the boars. He put the mothers and suckling babies in the middle of the pack. Around them he assembled the sows with no young and the young boars. And finally, at the outer edge of the pack, he placed the strong boars with their long, sharp tusks.

3

The tiger arrived with the morning sun, looking for a piglet for breakfast. When he saw the formation of boars he was stunned. He glared at them. The boars glared back. Stealthily he crept toward the group, his fangs bared. The carpenter's boar stepped forward and shook his head, and his long tusks gleamed in the pink morning sun. The rest of the large boars advanced with him. The tiger stared at this barricade of pointed ivory and thought of how easily their tusks could penetrate his beautiful coat. He reversed his crawl and disappeared into the forest.

"We have won!" said the boars. "Unity prevailed."

From then on, the pack of boars lived in their plentiful cave home, led by the wise, brave carpenter's boar.

# The Parakeet

**L**ONG AGO, on the coast not far from Mumbai, there lived a parakeet. He was a good parakeet and was faithful to his elderly parents, who could no longer gather food for themselves. Their eyes had dimmed and their flight had become slow and unsteady. They would stay in the nest and he would bring them fruit to eat. But the grove where he usually gathered fruit was frequented by many birds and monkeys, and good fruit had become harder and harder to find.

One day, from high on a mountain on the coast, the parakeet saw an island with a glowing grove of mango trees. It was a long flight, but he made it. The fruit on the island was abundant and delicious. The parakeet ate his fill and gathered more for his parents.

On his return to the nest, his father ate of the fruit and said, "Son, this is not from our regular grove. It is from the island in the ocean, is it not?

"Yes, Father, it is."

"Son, parakeets that go there do not live long. It is too dangerous. Please do not go to that island again!"

But the next day the son thought of the sweet, succulent fruit. He quickly forgot his promise to his father and again set off for the island. Once there, he ate and ate until he could eat no more. Then he saw a large ripe mango and plucked it for his parents. He flew for home, but with his full belly and carrying the heavy mango in his claws, he grew more and more tired. He sank ever closer to the water. In his weakness he did not notice a large wave moving his way. It swept him under the water, and he never rose again.

His poor parents, without the food he brought them, also perished. The parakeet's greed led not only to his own end but to the death of his loved ones as well.

# The Captive Monkey

**L**ONG AGO, on the edge of the Himalayas, a hunter saw a particularly fine monkey in the trees. Remembering that the king of Lucknow was very fond of monkeys, he captured the animal and took him to the palace. The king was very pleased and rewarded the hunter well. The monkey served the king for a long time and learned many tricks. He also learned the ways of men. At last, the king decided to reward the monkey for his service by giving him back his freedom.

He called the same hunter to his court and said, "Take this monkey to the spot where you captured him and set him free."

The hunter did as he was asked, and the monkey soon found his home troop. Most of the other monkeys did not remember him, but some of the older ones did. The young monkeys learned that he had been in the service of the king and were fascinated.

They came to him and said, "Please tell us what you learned living with men."

"No," said the monkey. "I would rather not."

"Oh, please!" begged the young monkeys. "What are the ways of men?"

"All right," said the monkey, "but you will not like it. 'Mine! Mine!' the men cry night and day. They know nothing of the temporary nature of wealth. 'Gold! Gold! Gold!' they shout, and never look to the holy truth. Women and men, alike in their greed, squawk, 'Rich clothes! Rich food! Rich jewels!' They know not the riches of the heart."

"Stop!" cried the young monkeys. "We can bear to hear no more!" They covered their ears and scampered high into the trees and never asked the monkey again about the ways of men.

# The Spotted Deer Brothers

 **L**ONG AGO,** near the kingdom of Magadha, there lived a large herd of spotted deer led by a wise old stag. As he was growing very infirm, he decided to split the herd, letting each of his sons, Luckie and Blackie, guide half of the deer.

It was harvest time in the fields near Magadha, and the thick golden stands of grain were a great temptation to the deer. The farmers, however, were determined to protect their crops, so they built staked pits, traps, and snares around their fields.

The wise old stag called his sons to him. "The fields are ripening," he said, "and the farmers have set their traps to catch the foolish deer who raid their crops. Every year many of our kind die trying reach those fields. Don't let your herds wander there. Take them to the mountains and forage for food where there is safety. When the crops are harvested you may return."

"As you say, Father," said the sons, and they bowed and took their leave. They gathered their respective herds and departed.

Huntsmen of the region knew of the annual migration of the deer to the mountains, and some gathered in hiding places along the main path. Still Blackie led his herd this way, because the path was wide and flat and offered the quickest way to the mountains. He moved them in the brightness of day, and when they passed the hunters, nearly a quarter of his herd was killed.

Luckie, on the other hand, took his herd by a small twisting path to the mountains. Their passage was slow and difficult, but it held no danger of hunters. Luckie moved the herd only in the night. They reached the lush mountain meadows without a single loss.

After several months in the mountains, knowing the crops had been harvested, the herds started back down to the valley. Blackie, having learned nothing, returned by the same route and again lost another quarter of his herd.

Luckie chose the same slow, safe route through the mountains and arrived with all his deer.

Upon seeing the herds, one that was large and healthy and the other small and tattered, the wise old stag exclaimed, "Blackie, you fool! Taking the easy way! You have led half your herd to their deaths while your brother has returned without losing a single deer."

The old stag gave charge of both herds to Luckie, and from then on the deer lived under his careful, wise leadership.

# The Quail and
# the Crow

ONG AGO, in the city of Mumbai, there lived a crow who survived by his wits. He scavenged on the carcasses of dead animals, picked bugs out of dung, and dug through trash for bits of rancid food.

One day he left the city and flew out over the forest in hope of finding something to eat. In a little clearing he saw a plump quail pecking away at the ground.

"What a fat, sleek bird," said the crow to himself. "She must have rich food to keep in such fine shape."

The crow flew down to the clearing and landed beside the quail, giving her quite a fright.

"Don't be afraid, dear friend," said the crow. "I only wish to talk with you."

"I was frightened by your suddenness," exclaimed the quail. "And also by your appearance: you are so skinny and ragged!"

"Yes," said the crow. "That is what I wanted to talk to you about. I am sure I do look skinny and ragged. I live my life in fear and struggle, fighting with jackals and vultures for bits of the dead. It is hard to grow fat when you must risk your life as I do to get a bite to eat. What do you eat to stay so plump and healthy?"

"Well," said the quail, "I eat seeds and grass. I pick my food from the ground. I fly only short distances, and live on what I find. I am content and at peace here in the forest. I have happiness and few cares. Come join me. Leave the city behind and find seeds with me, good crow."

The crow watched the quail as she pecked on the ground for tiny seeds.

"Thank you for your kind offer, dear quail," said the crow, "but

I am afraid the way of the quail is not the way of the crow. It is not in my nature to scratch at the earth."

With that, the crow took off and flew back toward the city, keeping a sharp eye out for carcasses below.

# The Snake, the Doctor, and the Boy

LONG AGO, in a dusty town north of Mumbai, there lived a doctor. He did not care much for his patients, but he did care for money. He overcharged his patients and lived in luxury. But even this was not enough. Soon he borrowed great sums of money and fell deeply into debt.

One morning as he was out walking in the town square, greatly worried about his finances, he saw a boy playing under a tree. He recognized the boy as the only son of the wealthiest man in town. He also saw a sleeping snake curled up deep in the crotch of the tree above the boy's head, about ten feet off the ground. "If that boy were to be bit on the hand by that snake," he thought, "his father would pay me a small fortune to save his life."

The doctor saw that there was no one near to witness his vile deed, and he said to the boy, "Dear child, there is a roll of rope coiled in the crotch of that tree you are under. Climb up and get it for me."

"Most certainly, sir," said the youth, and he began his climb. Just as the doctor hoped, he grasped the sleeping snake. But, thinking it was a rope, the boy immediately tossed it down to the doctor. The terrified snake wrapped himself around the man's neck and instinctively bit him, piercing a vein and injecting his poison.

The snake quickly slithered into the forest, and the doctor lay dead on the dusty ground—slain not through the fault of the snake but by his own greed.

# The Fish and
# the Holy Man

**L**ONG AGO, along the Ganges River, there was a small fishing village. One day, the men of the village were casting their nets into the river in hope of catching dinner for their families. Down the river swam a big fish, chasing a very beautiful female. The female fish was alert and saw the nets cast by the men, and she dodged at the last minute to avoid them. But the male, lost in his passion, swam directly into the trap. The joyful fishermen pulled in the great fish and heaved him upon the shore.

A holy man and his students had been watching the events unfold from high on the riverbank, and they saw the foolish behavior of the great fish.

The holy man said, "I must save this silly creature from such a fate."

He and his students walked down to the fishermen, and he said, "Dear friends, could you please let me have this great fish?"

The fishermen and the entire village greatly admired the holy man for his kindness and wisdom, and they said, without hesitation, "Surely, you may have the fish. Take it as a token of our appreciation for your goodness."

The holy man reached down and lifted the heavy fish, who was still flopping and struggling for his life. He took the fish a little distance downriver, out of sight of the fishermen, waded into the water, and released him. He then turned to his students and said, "Let this be a lesson to you. You may not be so lucky as this fish if you follow your passions. You may well be led into a net and then a frying pan."

19

# The Deer and
# the Hermit

**L**ONG AGO, in a valley of the Himalayas, there lived a hermit who survived on the wild fruits he found there. One day a beautiful fawn, having lost her mother, found her way to his hut. The hermit took the fawn in and fed and nurtured her. She grew into a beautiful doe, and the hermit loved her deeply. But after several years together, the deer fell ill from something she had eaten, and she soon died.

The hermit was heartbroken. He cried and cried. He cried for days.

A holy man came walking through the valley one day and heard the hermit weeping. "What is wrong, my friend?" he asked. "Why do you weep?"

Between sobs, the hermit told him the story of the fawn and her death.

"How long ago did your wonderful deer die?" asked the holy man.

"It was a week ago," replied the hermit.

"Grief is natural when death takes a loved one from us," said the holy man. "Tears can help us heal. But tears cannot turn back death. There is time to grieve and time to move on with our lives. You have shed enough tears for your fine friend. Cherish her memory, dry your tears, and live your life."

This comforted the hermit greatly. He shared a meal with the wise holy man, and went on with his life in the mountain valley.

# The Donkey and the Lion Skin

LONG AGO, in the villages south of Agra, there was a merchant who traveled from town to town, displaying his small wares for sale. He hauled the wares on the back of a worn-out donkey. The merchant was too cheap to buy grain for the poor old beast, so in each village he would throw a lion skin over the donkey and turn the animal loose in the barley fields. The villagers were always so frightened at the sight of a lion in their fields that they hid in their homes, while the donkey ate his fill.

One day, a farmer had had enough, and when he saw the lion he gathered his friends to drive him away. They rushed into the fields, pounding drums, blowing horns, and waving sticks.

The donkey was frightened out of his wits and gave out a loud "Hee-Haw!"

The farmer and his friends were astonished. "That is no lion!" cried the farmer. "That is a broken-down old donkey with a shabby lion skin draped over his back. And he is stealing my barley!"

The old donkey ran fast, but a few of the younger men came close enough to whack him on the backside, drawing an even louder "Hee-Haw!" Somehow, the poor beast still managed to outpace even the youngest villager.

The merchant witnessed what was going on and thought, "They will soon figure out whose donkey that is. I had better hurry from here."

He quickly wrapped his wares in a blanket and fled down the road in the direction of his donkey. The men knew at once that he must be the donkey's owner and the one responsible for stealing their barley.

"You wretch!" they shouted. "You overcharge us for your wares and then plunder our fields!"

The men easily overtook the merchant, who was slowed by his large burden, and they gave his backside far more strokes with their sticks than the donkey had received. Then they let him go, to hobble along the road after his beast.

The merchant and donkey never returned to the village again.

# The Owl, the Mynah Bird, and the Parrot

**L**ONG AGO, in the great city of Varanasi, there lived a king who had no children. This saddened him greatly, and one day, when he was walking in his palace gardens, he saw a strange-looking nest he had not noticed before. He called for one of his gardeners to bring a ladder, and he told the man to climb up to the nest.

"Is there anything in it?" shouted the king.

"Yes," replied the gardener. "There are three eggs, but it is strange. Each is of a different kind."

The king had the gardener retrieve the eggs, and he summoned his wisest advisers. The scholars examined the eggs and determined that one belonged to an owl, another to a mynah bird, and the last to a parrot.

The king said, "This is the answer to my prayers! The eggs shall hatch and the birds shall be my children."

The scholars were perplexed, but they took the eggs and kept them warm and protected them until they hatched.

The owl egg hatched first, and the scholars determined that the owlet was a boy. It was reported to the king, and he exclaimed, "A son!"

The second egg to hatch was that of the mynah bird. The hatchling was checked and found to be a girl. "A daughter!" cried the king.

The last hatchling to appear was that of the parrot. It too was a boy. "Two sons!" shouted the excited king.

He ordered that the chicks be cared for with extreme care, and quickly they grew to be fine young birds. The king ordered festivals to be held in their honor, and gave them every comfort. There were whispers in the king's court about the strangeness of his acts, and some thought he might be mad. The king heard of this and ordered

the birds to be brought to him one at a time and placed upon a golden stool for all to see.

First, the young owl was brought before the king. "It is said that my illustrious father wants to ask a question of me," said the handsome young owl. "Please do."

"Son," said the king, "what is the duty of a king?"

The owl paused for some time. Then he said, "A king must put away all lies, anger, and scorn. He must not be led astray by passion and lust. He must be devoted to what is right, and no matter what the consequences, never yield to evil thought. A king must be courageous and protect those who rely on him."

The young owl prince bowed to the king, who brimmed with pride. The courtiers were so astounded they could not speak.

Next the mynah bird was brought before the king and placed on the golden stool.

"Dearest father, you wish to speak with me?" said the lovely young bird.

Again the king asked, "What is the duty of a king?"

"Seek counsel only from the wisest of men," she said, "and only those who have forsworn gambling and drinking. Have direct knowledge of all transactions concerning the kingdom's money. Never decide important matters with haste. And always be truthful with people."

"My sweet daughter," said the king, "truer words were never spoken."

The people gathered around were equally impressed with the mynah bird and nodded their heads in appreciation.

Finally, the young parrot was brought before the king and placed on the stool. "My kind father, how good it is to see you," said the parrot.

The king said, "I have called you here, as I have your siblings, to ask you but one question: what is the duty of a king?"

The parrot took a long breath and said to his father, "A king must have the highest degree of learning, as he must possess great understanding to govern well. Fools make for very poor kings, and rapidly bring their lands to ruin. A king must not be lazy but full of energy to accomplish his many duties, so that his government may run smoothly. A king must put his subjects on a righteous path and guide them as a father."

The king shed tears of happiness. His advisers and courtiers were similarly moved by the remarkable display of wisdom by the three birds.

The king proclaimed to all those who had gathered, "These are my children indeed. They will join me on the throne of this kingdom, and together we will lead our people to great happiness."

And so they did for many, many years.

# The Geese and the Sun

**L**ONG AGO, on Lake Manasa in the Himalayas, there lived a flock of geese. The leader of the flock was a wise, remarkably large goose who guided the other geese on their flights and taught the young all the ways of the flock.

One day two young geese came to the leader and said, "We are young and strong. We win every race with our friends. We can fly as fast as the sun, and we will prove it."

The elder goose said, "While it might not seem so to you, the sun is the fastest of all things. Should you try to fly faster than the sun, you will surely perish."

The young geese, however, were full of themselves. They nodded to their leader, but off they went to plan their great adventure.

The next day they flew off to defeat the sun. They rose higher and higher in the sky. One of their mothers, who had heard of their plans, flew to the leader. "Dear sir, my son and another have gone to race with the sun. They are determined to win, but I fear for their safety!"

"You should well fear such foolishness," said the leader. "I will see if there is anything I can do."

With strong sweeps of his wings, he climbed into the air with great speed and soon overtook the young geese. One was about to collapse from his exertions. He fell from the sky, but the elder goose flew under him and caught him in his soft wings. He took him to the lake's edge and returned for the second goose. But the second young goose was stronger than the first, and when the elder goose came up beside him, he cried out, "I can do it! I can defeat the sun!" At that moment he too fainted and fell from the sky. Again the great leader swooped and caught him in his wings. He brought him to the lake and laid him gently on the ground beside his friend.

The young geese were nursed back to health by their mothers. When they were feeling better, they went to the elder goose. "You saved our lives," said the humbled young geese. "We are forever in your debt."

"You may repay your debt," said the elder, "by following common sense when you hear it."

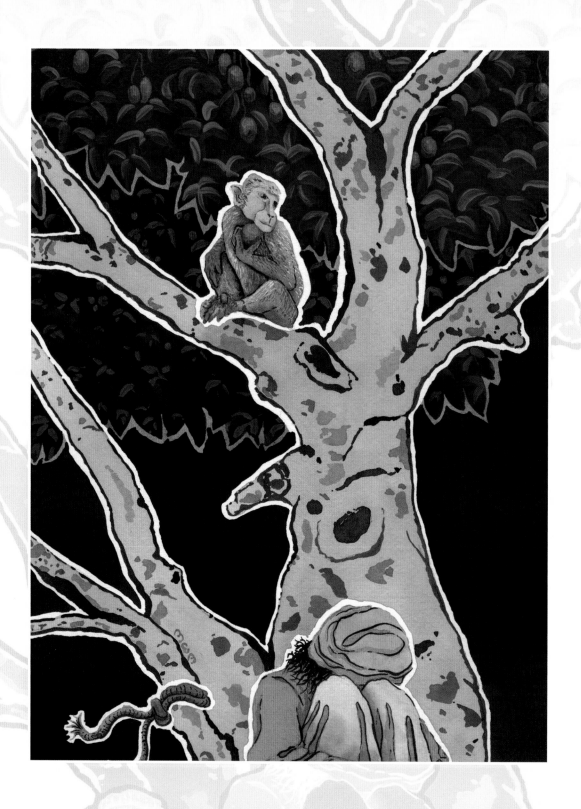

# The Monkey and the Snake Charmer

**L**ONG AGO, in the great city of Varanasi, there was a cruel snake charmer who abused a monkey in his act. After giving the monkey a drug to protect him from the snake's poison, he made the monkey play with the snake until he was bitten. The audience was both amazed and appalled.

The man beat the monkey often and fed him little, and the monkey became sickly and depressed. One night, after tying the poor creature to a mango tree, the man fell asleep against its trunk. The monkey worked and worked on the ropes that bound him. They were very tight, and his ankle bled, but finally he was free. He threw the ropes aside and quickly scurried high into the mango tree. The monkey ate a delicious ripe mango and tossed the pit down on the head of the snake charmer.

The man awoke with a start. He looked up into the tree and saw his monkey far up in the branches. "Get down here this minute, or I'll beat you like I have never beaten you before!" cried the man.

"And how would you get ahold of me?" said the monkey.

The man saw the truth in this and changed his approach.

"You are like a son to me, dear monkey. Come down and I will never beat you again. I promise."

"You promise?" said the monkey. "What good are promises from a wicked man? I will live now in the trees and eat sweet mangos."

And he swung from tree to tree until the snake charmer was out of sight.

# The Elephant,
# the Carpenters,
# and the King

**L**ONG AGO, deep in the forest north of Varanasi, a large bull elephant roamed. One day he accidentally stepped upon a large splinter of wood, which lodged deeply in his foot and became infected. The elephant grew increasingly ill and at last could only lie on his side and moan. Some carpenters, who often came into that part of the forest to gather timber for their work, heard the deep moaning of the sick elephant. They found the suffering elephant and took mercy on him, carefully removing the splinter, cleansing the wound with warm water, and caring for the elephant until he was healed.

The elephant was so grateful to be out of pain that he said to the carpenters, "I would have surely died in agony had you not cared for me with such compassion. From now on I will help you with your work."

So the elephant joined the men. He uprooted trees, rolled them for trimming, and carried the logs to the river. He worked happily until, in his old age, it became too difficult for him. He asked his son—a beautiful, strong, white elephant—to take over his work, and to continue to repay the carpenters for saving his life. His son was happy to do so and set to the task immediately. He was every bit as good of a worker as his father, and the carpenters grew equally fond of him.

News of this wonderful white elephant spread to the city and came to the attention of the king, who loved elephants. He decided that he must own the great beast. He and a large group of his attendants went to the forest and found the carpenters at work with the elephant. The carpenters were honored that the king had come to see them and said, "Sire, what a joy to have you here. What wood can we supply you with?"

"No," said the king, "I come not for wood but for your white elephant."

Though they were sad to lose their friend, the carpenters could not disobey the king. "He is yours," they said, bowing deeply.

But the white elephant would not budge an inch. He said, "You must pay my friends a fair price if I am going with you."

The king gave the carpenters a rich reward for the elephant, but still the elephant would not move. Again he spoke. "And you must provide my companions with new clothes for themselves and their families."

The king happily did as he was asked, and so the elephant accompanied him to the city and to the spacious, comfortable palace stables. Soon the elephant became the king's favorite and the only elephant he would ride. They grew so close that the king came to care for the elephant as a dear friend, and the elephant was completely devoted to the king.

Years passed, and one day the king became gravely ill and died. All the members of the court agreed that the white elephant should not be told of the king's death, lest it break his heart as it had broken the heart of the king's young wife, who had just given birth to the king's only son.

The ruler of a nearby kingdom heard of the king's death and launched his troops against the leaderless kingdom. The court of the dead king was frightened and at a loss for what to do. Finally, one of the advisers beseeched the queen. "Please," he said, "tell the white elephant of the king's death and seek his help."

The queen agreed, and she took her son to the elephant. She told the elephant the terrible news, and large tears rolled from his eyes. "Now there are enemy troops gathered outside the city walls," she said.

The elephant reached down and lifted the infant king with his trunk. He held the child tenderly and then returned him to his mother.

"For my dead friend and for my new king, I will send these invaders back to their lands," he said.

The men dressed the elephant in battle armor and opened the city gates for him. He charged into the enemy lines with such trumpeting and wildness that the soldiers ran for their lives. He destroyed and trampled their entire camp. Then the elephant found the fleeing ruler of the invaders and, grabbing him with his trunk, held the terrified man over his head as he returned to the palace. There he laid the vanquished ruler at the feet of the queen and the infant king. Many at the court shouted for the man's death, but the elephant stopped them and said to the trembling man, "Go back to your kingdom and stay there. Do not presume to attack those you think are weak, as it may not be so." The humbled, defeated man fled with his troops.

Time passed and the young king took the throne, and ruled with justice and compassion. The white elephant grew old and was adored and loved by all in the kingdom.

# The Monkeys and the Water Ogre

 **L**ONG AGO, in a forest not far from the city of Gaya, there was a beautiful small lake. In that lake there lived a nasty water ogre. When animals came to drink from the lake, the ogre would swiftly grab them, pull them under the water, and eat them.

One day a troop of monkeys, led by an old wise chief, passed near the lake, looking for food and water. The monkey chief had taught his troop not to eat any fruit or drink any water they came across in the forest until he had judged it safe. When the monkeys happened upon the beautiful little lake, although the water looked clear and delicious and the monkeys were very thirsty, they remembered their leader's warning.

When the old monkey arrived he asked the others if they had tested the water. They were waiting for him, they said.

"Quite right and sensible of you," said the chief.

Along the lake's edge he found a suitable spot for drinking, but he noticed that while many animal tracks led down to the water, none came back.

"Surely," said the chief, "this lake is the haunt of a water ogre who eats all who come to drink."

The old monkey told his troop to sit at a good distance from the shore and wait. The ogre, who observed all this from the depths of the lake, grew impatient and rose from the water.

"What are you waiting for? Come satisfy your thirst!" he cried with a deep voice.

"Are you not the ogre of this lake?" asked the chief.

"Yes, I most certainly am,"

"Do you not eat all who come here to drink?" asked the chief.

"To be sure," said the ogre. "I eat everything that comes to these

39

waters, whether small birds or water buffalo. And I shall eat all of you too!"

"You will not eat any us," said the old monkey, "and we will drink our fill."

The wise monkey led his troop to a cluster of very tall hollow canes growing not far from the lake.

"Each of you shall take a cane, break off the top, and blow any fiber out of the center," he said, and he showed them how to do so. The monkeys quickly completed their task, and soon they all clutched hollow canes, five or six feet in length. The chief took the troop back to the shore of the lake, and, well beyond of the reach of the ogre, he sucked the clear fresh water with his cane straw. All of his troop did the same, and they satisfied their thirst.

The ogre watched in disbelief. When the troop was about to depart, the old monkey turned to him and said, "You will have to wait for less cautious creatures for your dinner today."

# The Golden Peacock
# and the Hunter

**L**ONG AGO, not far from Agra, a wild peahen hatched a most unusual chick. Its color was that of burnished gold. As the young peacock grew, the color deepened and became even richer. He was a vision of pure beauty.

One day, the peacock caught sight of his own reflection in a pond. "Oh my," he thought. "It is not good to be so beautiful. Certainly men will wish to capture me."

He traveled in search of a place where men could not find him, and came to a lotus-covered lake in the remote foothills of the Himalayas. There he established his favorite perch in an enormous banyan tree on the lake's edge. He was content in this place, which was most fitting for one so sublime.

One day a hunter discovered the valley of the peacock. He caught a glimpse of the golden bird and could not believe his eyes. But then, as quickly as the bird appeared, he vanished. The man hunted and hunted but could not find the elusive peacock. When the man returned to his family he told his eldest son of what he had seen. The son was an even better hunter than his father and swore that he would trap the peacock and sell him at the king's court. For years, he hunted for the bird, with no success. Now and then he would catch glimpses of him, but he was never close enough to capture him.

One afternoon an idea came to the son, which he was sure would work. He bought the most beautiful peahen he could find. He went to the lotus-covered lake, where he knew the golden peacock lived, and staked the peahen to the ground and carefully set snares all around her. Then he waited.

The golden bird did at last arrive, drawn to the lovely peahen

as a bee is drawn to a pollen-rich flower. A snare caught his leg and he was swept upside down, hanging by his foot.

For the first time, the hunter could look closely at the peacock. He was dumbfounded by his beauty. His color, size, tail, and even his calm composure in the snare were beyond his experience. The hunter suddenly felt what a terrible injustice it would be to take this creature out of his glorious valley and sell him as a captive. He wished to release the bird but was fearful of approaching him with a knife, as the peacock's huge claws could still do great damage. He decided to shoot an arrow through the snare's rope and free the bird.

When the peacock saw the hunter nock an arrow in his bow, he spoke to him. "I will be worth much more alive than dead," he said. "Put down your bow and you will be rich."

"I will not kill you but free you," said the hunter.

"You have been pursuing me for years, enduring many hardships," said the peacock. "Why would you wish to free me now?"

"Because I have seen how cruel it would be to keep a bird as remarkable as you in captivity." The hunter went up to the bird and gently released him from the snare.

The peacock had never encountered a man such as this. He asked, "If it is unjust to take my freedom, what of all the other birds who may be less beautiful? Is it just to place them in cages?"

"No," said the man. "It is not just, and I will have no part of it from this day forward."

"Such goodness," said the peacock, "has countless rewards, far beyond gold and riches."

The hunter released the peahen as well, to stay and become the peacock's mate. He returned to his home and took up his uncle's trade of pottery. Thus he made his living and cared for the needs of his family, and with any extra money he had, he bought captive birds and set them free.

# The Lion and the Tiger

**L**ONG AGO, at the foot of a mountain, there lived a lion and a tiger in the same large cave. It was very unusual for such beasts to live together, but they had become friends and most of the time they got along. A hermit lived in a small cave nearby and was likewise friends with the formidable cats.

One day, the lion and the tiger were sitting outside their cave, engaged in a dispute about the weather.

"No!" said the tiger. "You are wrong! The cold comes with the waning of the moon!"

"I told you, foolish tiger," roared the lion, "it is always with the waxing of the moon that the cold comes to this mountain!"

The two argued and argued until finally they decided to ask the hermit to settle the matter.

"Dear hermit," they called to their friend in his cave. "Please come out and settle this for us."

The hermit appeared and asked what troubled them. The lion and the tiger both put forward their cases.

The hermit thought for a long while, knowing that to keep the peace required a solution that would offend neither of the great cats.

"It is not the waning or the waxing of the moon that brings the cold, but the wind," he said. "Whether the moon grows larger or smaller matters not to the wind, so you are both completely right."

The lion and the tiger saw the wisdom of the hermit's words, smiled at one another, and returned to their cave as friends once more.

# The Parrot Brothers

**L**ONG AGO, in the hills south of Bodh Gaya, two parrot chicks were hatched in a low nest. Their mother was out gathering food for them when a boy from the village spotted the little birds and stole them from their nest.

He gave the first chick to a small community of holy men. The second he sold to a band of thieves. Thus the two brother birds were raised in very different circumstances.

One day a prince, hunting in the forest, became lost. Hungry and forlorn, he curled up beside a tree to sleep for the night. The parrot from the band of robbers came upon the prince and thought gleefully, "Look at his rich clothes and fat purse. I will hurry back to the camp and bring my friends to take everything he has."

Just then, the parrot of the holy men saw the prince huddled by the tree. He flew down to him and said, "Dear sir, may I help you? This is a dangerous forest. Thieves live not far from here."

"Kind parrot," said the prince, "I am certainly lost and would be most grateful for any help you might give."

"With pleasure," said the parrot, and he guided the prince to the road leading to the city. The prince was very thankful. He gave the parrot a large golden coin as a reward for his goodness.

The parrot flew back to the village and told the holy men the story of the lost prince in the woods, and he gave the men the valuable coin. The holy men were delighted. Now they had enough money for food and offerings. They praised the parrot and gave him an extra helping of fruit for his breakfast.

Meanwhile, the other parrot guided the band of thieves to where the prince had slept. Finding no one, the thieves grew furious with the parrot for waking them. They beat the parrot and left him in the forest.

So it was that two parrots from the same mother were made very different by the company they kept.

# The She-Goat
# and the Jackals

**L**ONG AGO, on the slopes of the Himalayas, there dwelled a herd of wild mountain goats. A jackal and his wife lived in a den in the same area, and the jackal craved to eat the goats. But the herd was led by a very wise she-goat who always kept the goats, young and old, out of harm's reach.

The jackal hatched a plot to kill the she-goat, and put the rest of the herd at his mercy.

"This is what you must do," said the jackal to his wife. "You must go to the she-goat and weep and tear at your hair, and tell her I have died. Beg her to grieve with you and to help bury my body. I will lie still, and when she is within reach she will be our first goat dinner."

Weeping and sobbing, the jackal's wife approached the she-goat. "My dear, sweet husband has died," she said. "Please come and cry with me and help me bury his remains. I cannot manage on my own."

But the she-goat knew the ways of jackals. "Your husband was cruel-minded, and I am afraid," she said. "I cannot come."

"He is dead and can do you no harm," the jackal's wife said. "Please help me, his poor wife, as you would want to be helped."

At last, out of compassion, the she-goat agreed, but she made the jackal's wife travel ahead of her on the path, and she kept a careful watch for danger. As they neared the limp body of the jackal, he could not resist opening one eye a tiny bit. The wary she-goat saw the flicker of the jackal's eye and cried out, "You wicked jackals! He lives!" And she bounded back down the path.

The jackal was furious. "Your dull wits have frightened her away!"

"My dull wits!" replied his wife. "It was your eager eye that sent her down the path!"

Neither of them was to dine on goat that day. And by the caution of the wise she-goat, they never would.

# The Hawks, the Osprey, the Turtle, and the Lion

ONG AGO, near a beautiful little lake in the woods not far from Gaya, there lived two hawks, an osprey, a turtle, and a lion. One day, the hawk's wife, who had been doing some thinking, asked the hawk, "Whom do we have for friends?"

"Well, no one comes to mind," said the hawk.

"We should have friends," said the wife. "We can help them, and they can help us."

"Yes," said the hawk, "you are absolutely right. It is a good thing. I will seek out some friends for us."

First the hawk flew to the great osprey who lived in a dead tree stretched out over the lake. The hawk landed on the edge of the osprey's large nest and said, "Dear Osprey, I would like to be your friend and help you when needed, and you may help me when I am in need."

The osprey thought this over and said, "Yes, Hawk, that is a fine idea. One never knows when assistance might be needed."

The hawk then flew to the turtle who lived on an island in the middle of the lake. He was an enormous turtle and was basking in the sun on a boulder that stretched into the lake.

The hawk landed on the edge of the boulder and said, "Good Turtle, may I speak with you on a matter of importance?"

The turtle agreed, and after the hawk asked for his friendship, the turtle said, "Surely, it is an excellent plan to have friends."

Finally, the hawk flew to the north end of lake where the lion lived in a cave not far from the shore. The hawk landed on a tree near the cave's entrance, and, being a bit fearful of the great cat, he called out in a quiet voice, "Great Lion, oh, Great Lion, are you home?"

The lion came out of the cave and looked around but saw no one.

"Up here, Great One," said the hawk. "May I ask you a question?"

The lion was a mighty beast but also a wise one. He said to the hawk, "Noble Hawk, ask your question."

The hawk once again asked for friendship.

The lion listened thoughtfully and replied, "I am so glad you asked me. I would be happy to be your friend and a friend to all your friends."

The hawk was delighted with the success of his efforts, and he flew home and told his wife, who was equally pleased. The months passed and the new friends visited often and enjoyed the company of one another. In the spring, the hawk's wife hatched two eggs, and the chicks began to grow. The hawk and his wife hunted for food and were proud of their fine offspring.

One day, a group of teenage boys from a nearby village came to the lake to fish, swim, and play. They rested on the shore under the tree in which the two hawk chicks were staying, waiting for their parents to return from a hunt. The boys, who were bothered by mosquitos, made a smoky fire to keep the bugs away. The smoke rose up the tree and into the hawks' nest. The chicks, who could not yet fly, began to squawk as the smoke stung their eyes.

The boys heard the young birds and one of them said, "We have no fish, but we could have roasted fowl for dinner!"

The boys began piling wood on the fire, determined to burn the tree down to get the young birds. Just then, the hawk and his wife returned from their hunt. Seeing their chicks in danger, they began diving at the boys to prevent them from feeding the fire. But the boys took long sticks and beat the hawks when they swooped down. Soon the hawks were exhausted, and the wife's left wing was nearly broken. They landed in a nearby tree, and the quick-thinking wife said to her husband, "Go! Fly to the osprey for help!"

The hawk flew at great speed and told the osprey of their plight. The osprey said, "We shall leave at once!"

As the osprey was reaching the hawk's tree he dove into the lake and came up with cupped wings full of water. He flew to the fire and, dumping the water, extinguished it. This infuriated the boys, and they rebuilt the fire even larger. The osprey again and again tried to quench the flames, but each time the boys beat him off with their sticks and he too became so battered he had to stop.

Again the wife said to her husband, "Hurry! Go to our turtle friend and ask him to help!"

The hawk quickly found the turtle, who swam with surprising speed to the site of the fire. He emerged from the water pushing a huge mound of mud before him. He spread the mud over the fire and put it out.

The boys were again enraged, but the cruelest among them spoke up, "We may not have fowl for dinner, but that great turtle has more than enough meat for all of us."

The boys took off their shirts to form a rope by which to flip the turtle over. But they could hardly lift him, and the turtle slowly dragged them all into the lake. The boys came up choking on the water, and sputtering with anger.

"This time," they said, "the chicks will be ours!"

Again they built the fire, even bigger.

"It is our last chance!" screamed the wife to her husband. "Fly to our lion friend and plead for his help!"

The hawk found the lion, but he did not have to plead. When the lion heard the tale, he charged through the trees with a roar that filled the forest and echoed over the lake. The boys heard the terrible sounds and were filled with fear. They fled the fire and ran with all their might back to their village.

The osprey and turtle soon put out the fire and stood at the foot of the tree with the lion. The hawks perched on their nest and lovingly soothed their chicks, who were sick from the smoke but still very much alive.

The wife wept with happiness. "Oh dear friends, you have saved our chicks! This is true friendship. You have put yourselves in danger for our good. We will do the same for you at a moment's notice."

And so, for many years to come, the animals lived in friendship.

# The Goat and the Panther

**L**ONG AGO, in the mountains of the Himalayas, a holy man sat on a high crag and witnessed the following encounter.

A young goat was making her way along a narrow mountain trail when she turned a bend and found herself face-to-face with a muscular black panther. The panther had been a terror to the herd and possessed a reputation for meanness. The young goat knew well that on the narrow path she could not outrun the cat.

"Well hello, Uncle," she said in a most pleasant voice. "How lovely to see you this fine morning. My mother sends her regards."

"This little goat tries to fool," thought the panther. "Well, I am no fool." He growled at her. "You have trodden on my tail. Calling me 'Uncle' will not save you from becoming my breakfast!"

The young goat kept her cool composure and replied, "Now, Uncle. You sit on the path facing me and your tail is behind you. How could I have stepped on it?"

"You little wretch!" scowled the panther. "My tail can stretch across the continents and the seas. You could not fail to tread on it!"

As her politeness was not working, the little goat changed her strategy.

"Yes, your evil tail is long and your disposition is vile. But I did not walk here. I flew through the sky and could not have stepped on your filthy tail!"

"Oh yes," said the sly panther. "You flew, and as you did you frightened away the deer I was stalking. Now you must take its place."

The panther pounced on the little goat and devoured her.

The holy man, who had heard every word that was spoken, shook his head with sadness and thought, "The little goat was clever and quick with her mind, but such qualities do not always win over the powerful and the hungry."

# The Singula Bird
# and the Monkey

LONG AGO, in a southern valley of the Himalayas, there lived a singula bird who had grown into a fine, large, multicolored specimen of his species. He had built a remarkable nest high in a tree. The nest was densely constructed on all sides, with an arched roof. One day, a heavy rain began to fall. The bird sat serenely in his wonderful nest without a drop of water reaching him. A few branches below him, a monkey sat drenched with rain, his teeth chattering in the cold. And at the base of the tree sat a hermit, dry and warm in his hut. The hermit was watching the rain, the bird, and the monkey.

"Monkey," said the bird. "Why do you sit out in the wet cold when you have hands and feet like that of men who can build so many fine structures for their comfort? I have but a beak and claws, and yet I have managed this fine abode."

The monkey squinted his wet eyes at the bird and said with irritation, "I may have hands and feet like a man, but I was given neither his wit nor his skills."

"Well," said the bird, "maybe you have not applied yourself to use your gifts."

The monkey was irate. "Yes," he said, "maybe there is something I can do with these hands!" He sprung at the bird, who quickly darted for an upper branch. The monkey landed on his nest and tore it apart until every stick lay scattered on the forest floor.

"You were right, Bird," sneered the monkey. "These hands are very useful tools." And he swung from tree to tree until he was out of sight.

The hermit, who had witnessed the entire episode, said these few words: "It is best to leave the ill-tempered to their own affairs."

# The Pigeon
# and the Crow

LONG AGO, in the ancient city of Varanasi, there lived a pigeon who had a comfortable home in a basket generously hung in the kitchen by the cook of a wealthy merchant. The pigeon flew out over the city every day to scratch the earth and find seeds for his meals. A crow began to follow him, but the pigeon did not know why. One evening, the crow followed him all the way home to the kitchen.

"Why do you follow me?" the pigeon asked the crow. "We do not eat the same things."

The crow, who had smelled the fish and meat of the kitchen, hoped to fill his stomach by pretending to be friendly with the pigeon. "I admire you so," said the crow. "I just want to be your companion."

For several days the birds flew about the city, the pigeon scratching for his grass seeds and the crow picking through cow dung for insects. The kindly cook hung out a second basket for his pigeon's new friend and thought little of it.

One morning the cook brought a large fish into the kitchen for the merchant's evening meal. The crow was overwhelmed by the aroma and decided that on this day he would feast. "Oh, my stomach," groaned the crow. "I am too ill to go out with you today, dear pigeon. You go without me."

"I have never heard of crows having stomachaches," said the pigeon with suspicion. "You behave yourself, or trouble will be yours." And off went the pigeon to seek his seeds.

The cook began to prepare a stew and cut the fish into large pieces as the crow lay low in his basket. When the cook stepped outside the kitchen for some fresh air, the crow made his move. He flew down to the table. But just as he was about to gulp a large piece of

59

fish, his tail bumped a kettle lid, which gave a loud clang. The cook quickly returned and saw the crow's mischief. "What a thankless creature you are!" said the cook as he brought his meat cleaver down on the crow's neck. He tossed the crow's remains into a basket and returned to making the meal.

Later, when the pigeon returned from his day's work, he saw the crow's limp body in the basket. "Oh, you greedy crow," he said with a sigh. "You did not listen to me, and now you have come to this sad end."

That night the cook threw the basket, crow and all, onto the garbage pile.

# The Jackal and
# the Merchant

ONG AGO, in a village not far from Varanasi, a feast was held to honor the local gods. In their revelry the townspeople scattered leftover food and even pots of strong drink in the streets and alleys. A jackal had been watching the wild celebration from the bushes at the edge of the village. Late at night, when the last of the villagers had gone to their homes, the jackal crept into town and began to dine. He ate all the food and cleaned out every pot of beer. He was so bloated and drunk he crawled into a bush by a hut and fell into a deep sleep. When he awoke with a splitting headache in the bright sunlight, people were already milling about the streets.

The jackal thought, "I am in trouble now. I cannot make my way out of the village without being seen, and if I *am* seen the villagers will beat me with sticks. They most certainly do not like jackals."

Soon a merchant was nearing the bush in which the jackal was hiding. The jackal recognized the man as someone who had a reputation for greed. An idea came to him.

"Merchant, come here please," whispered the jackal as the man walked by.

The curious merchant walked closer to the bush and said, "Who is hiding in there?"

"I have a hundred pieces of gold hidden not far from the village," said the jackal, "and if you take me there wrapped in your robe it is all yours."

"A hundred pieces of gold," thought the merchant. "I will be a rich man." He agreed to the plan, wrapped the jackal in his robe, and followed the animal's directions out of town.

Finally, when they were a good distance from the village, the jackal said, "This is the place. I will dig up the gold and place it on

your robe so you can take it back to town. Go find a sturdy stick with which to carry the bundle."

The merchant hurried away. He searched and searched until he found just the right stick with which to carry his fortune, and he hastened back to the robe. To his surprise, it was not a fortune of gold that lay upon the robe, but a pile of steaming excrement.

"There is your treasure, Merchant," called the jackal from the edge of the woods. "Take it back to the village and show all your friends." He ran deep into the woods, chuckling all the way.

The greedy merchant shook the filth from his robe and slowly walked back to the village.

# The Elephant
# and the Thieves

**L**ONG AGO, in the great city of Varanasi, there lived a king who kept a stable of elephants. He had a favorite elephant named Damsel. She was a kind and gentle elephant who was good to all her fellow elephants and her keepers.

It came to be that a group of thieves began to use the little room adjoining her stall to plan their crimes. Damsel could hear every word they said as they talked late into the night, cursing, laughing, and plotting their evil deeds. This went on for weeks and months. Damsel's keepers began to notice a change coming over her. She became surly and no longer obeyed her trainer. She even started to trumpet, rear up, and stomp about. When she was with other elephants she no longer treated them with kindness, but poked them and pushed them out of her way.

The keepers of the king's elephants were all dumbfounded by this, and the king himself was greatly concerned. One night the king's guards discovered the thieves in their room and chased them out of the palace grounds. One of the king's finest advisers, who heard of this event, went to the king. "I believe I know what is wrong with Damsel," he said.

"Do tell me," said the king.

"I have just been told that ruffians have been using the room next to Damsel's stall," the adviser said. "I believe their harsh, crude words and rough behavior have influenced your gentle elephant, and she has adopted their bad behavior."

"What can be done?!" exclaimed the king.

"I have a plan," said the wise adviser.

The adviser gathered together a group of sages, good men, and religious scholars and had them meet nightly in the room beside Damsel's stall. Night after night, and week after week, they spoke of nothing but kindness, compassion, forgiveness, and duty. And little by little, Damsel returned to her previous goodness. She became even more gentle and kind.

The adviser reported all of this to the king, who was so delighted he rewarded the adviser generously and praised him. "The company we keep," he said, "shapes who we are."

# The Goose
# and Her Son

LONG AGO, in a lush forest north of the city of Gaya, there was a spacious freshwater lake dappled with lotus flowers. The lake was the favorite stopping place for many birds, including a flock of geese led by a kind, wise elder goose. She always did her best to guide her flock to safe waters, where the food was plentiful and predators were few.

The most dangerous of all predators were the fowlers, men who caught birds and took them back to the city to sell as meat. A particularly skilled fowler heard of this great lake with its many flocks of birds and found his way there. He set carefully concealed snares just beneath the water to catch geese and ducks.

News had reached the elder goose that more and more hunters were starting to come to the lake, so she planned to fly her flock past it. But the other geese were heartbroken. They yearned for the lake's beauty and its delicious fish and snails and insects. She finally agreed to let the flock alight on the lake and found a quiet, secluded place she thought would be safe from men. Unfortunately, the skilled fowler had picked just this spot for his traps. As the elder goose was landing on the water, a snare caught her foot. The speed of her descent pulled the snare tight against her leg. It was so well set she knew that neither she nor any of her flock could remove it. She also knew if she alerted the other geese they would panic and more would be caught. It will be better, she thought, to let them feed awhile and then send them quietly on their way.

After some time, when all the geese were well fed and happy, she said to her flock, "It is time to go. Swim quietly to the middle of the lake and take flight to the south. I will stay here and feed a little longer."

The flock followed her guidance and flew for the south. After

some time, the son of the elder goose noticed that his mother had still not joined them. He grew worried and turned back. He found her exactly where they had left her, and discerned the situation.

"Mother, are you snared?" cried the son as he landed.

"I am," she said calmly. "And why did you land here? You could have been snared as well."

"Mother!" lamented the son. "I cannot leave you to a fowler. I cannot abandon you. I would rather die with you."

At this time the fowler came creeping along the shore and saw the two geese in the area of his snares. At first he was pleased to have caught them both, but then he saw that while one goose was definitely trapped, the other swam freely. This perplexed him, and he thought, "In all my years I have never seen a free goose stay with a snared one." He crawled closer to the geese and stood up, expecting the unbound goose to fly away. It did no such thing but swam closer to the captive bird.

"Fly away!" said the mother to her son. "Please fly away! You will be caught as well!"

"I cannot," he said. "If I leave, my heart will break and I will die anyway. I will stay with you to the end."

The fowler listened to this, and his heart ached with sympathy. He said, "I have never seen or heard such devotion. Never did I realize that birds could have such feelings."

He waded into the lake and gently cut the snare holding the mother's leg. "Please go," he said. "You and your son must catch up with your flock. May you lead long and happy lives."

With gratitude to the fowler, the two geese rose from the lake and swiftly joined the flock.

The fowler walked home, wondering deeply if he could continue his trade of taking the lives of such noble creatures.

# The Monkeys and the Village Fruit Tree

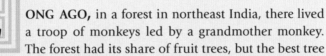

LONG AGO, in a forest in northeast India, there lived a troop of monkeys led by a grandmother monkey. The forest had its share of fruit trees, but the best tree of all stood at the center of a small village. This tree produced the finest fruit—sweet, succulent, and large. Every year the monkeys would sneak into the village during the night and eat their fill of the tree's fruit. The people grew tired of the thieving monkeys and built a tall fence around the tree and posted guards whenever the fruit was ripe.

One day a monkey was sent to spy on the tree in the village. He saw the fence and the guards and returned to tell the others.

The grandmother monkey said, "If people are angered they can be very dangerous. They mean to protect that tree, and we should stay away. There are other fruit trees in the forest."

But a group of young monkeys was eager for that special fruit, and they plotted to raid the tree. "If we wait until very late at night, the guards will fall asleep," one of them said. "We can easily scale the fence and eat our fill."

That evening the young monkeys crept into the village. As predicted, late at night the guards dozed off. The monkeys, ever so quietly, scaled the fence and began to gorge themselves on the candy-like fruit. Suddenly one of the guards awoke. He saw the monkeys and sounded the alarm. Villagers rushed from their huts with clubs, knives, and bows and arrows. They surrounded the fence.

One monkey, who had been too afraid to scale the fence, watched the scene from the edge of the village. He hurried back and informed the grandmother monkey of the disaster.

"Just as I feared," she said. "Why didn't those young fools listen to my advice? Well, let's go see if we can get them out of this mess."

When they arrived at the outskirts of the village, the villagers were shaking their weapons at the terrified monkeys in the tree.

"Fortunately for us, people are easily distracted," said the wise old grandmother monkey.

She stealthily made her way to a hut where a cooking fire burned. She took a firebrand and carried it to a vacant hut on the far edge of the village. There she tossed the burning log onto the hut's thatched roof. The dry thatch exploded into flames. The villagers who had gathered around the tree saw the flames and cried, "Fire! Fire!" They ran to the burning hut to extinguish the flames before the fire spread to other homes. Seeing their opportunity, the young monkeys in the fruit tree scrambled back over the fence and into the forest.

When the whole troop was joined together again, the young monkeys approached their grandmother and, with downcast eyes, said, "Oh Grandmother, from this day forward we will always follow your wise guidance."

# The Golden Deer and
# the Merchant's Son

**L**ONG AGO, in Varanasi, there was a wealthy merchant who worked hard and amassed a small fortune. He had a son whom he spoiled terribly all through his life. The merchant died and left his fortune to his son. The son knew nothing but drinking, dancing, feasting, and gambling. In a short time the fortune was gone and he had fallen deeply in debt. The son sank into depression. He decided he would rather be dead than poor. He told all his creditors that he had buried the family wealth on the banks of the Ganges and invited them all there to claim their debts. When the creditors had gathered he threw himself into the river to drown. A great current grabbed him and pulled him downriver, but suddenly the son changed his mind. He wanted to live. He struggled in the swift water and called out with pitiful cries.

Nearby, in a secluded grove along the banks of the Ganges, there lived an extraordinary animal: a golden deer with antlers like silver and eyes like jewels. The deer heard the cries from the river and felt compassion for the drowning man. He leapt into the powerful current of the river and swam to the man. Taking him on his back, he brought him to shore. The deer nursed the man back to health with fruit, and he made for him a dry bed of grass on which to rest.

When the man had recovered he said to the deer, "I have never seen such a beast as you! Your beauty is surely matched by your kindness."

The deer replied, "Now that you have recovered, I will show you to the road to Varanasi, and you can return to your life. But you must promise not to tell anyone of my existence, as there are those who would wish to make a golden deer their own."

The man promised. He planned to disguise himself, so as not to be discovered by his creditors, and to begin a new life in the city.

At this time the queen of Varanasi had a vivid dream. She dreamt of a golden deer who taught with great wisdom. So real was this dream, the queen became convinced that the deer must actually exist. She went to the king. "I must have this golden deer teach me the truth!" she said. "There is no point to my life if this deer is not a part of it."

The king said, "If such a deer exists, we will find him." He ordered that notices be posted throughout the city and countryside. The notices promised a large reward for information leading to the golden deer.

As the merchant's son was making his way back into the city, disguised in the clothes of a peasant, one of the king's men passed him on a royal elephant, from which he loudly proclaimed the search for the golden deer and the reward. The merchant's son thought of the life of ease he had lived in the past and the life of poverty that was in his future.

He rushed to the man on the elephant and cried, "I know! I know where this creature lives!" He was taken immediately to the palace. The queen and king were overjoyed with the news. They quickly organized a huge group of soldiers to capture the deer.

The merchant's son guided the king and his army to the grove and they encircled it. The deer, seeing that he was trapped, emerged from the brush and slowly walked toward the king. The king was frightened of the large, graceful beast, and he drew an arrow in his bow.

"I mean you no harm, great king," said the deer. His voice was so beautiful that the king could only drop his bow and stare in wonder.

"Tell me, sir," said the deer, "who told you where to find me?"

The king pointed to the merchant's son, who was trying to hide behind a tree.

"Yes," said the deer, "I thought so. He is the man whose life I saved only days ago and who promised not to speak of me or tell of my location."

The king became furious. He ordered the man to be executed on the spot.

"No," said the deer. "Do not kill him. He is but a weak and greedy man. There are many of his kind. Let him go. He will bring suffering on himself to pay for his ill deeds."

The king was amazed at the wisdom, compassion, and grace of the golden deer.

"Great deer," said the king, "my wife has dreamed that you are to teach her the truth. May she and I come to your grove and listen to your teachings? I will post guards around the grove to keep you safe."

The deer agreed, and the king and queen came often to hear his wise words. The king was so pleased that he told the deer, "Ask for anything you wish, my dear friend, and it will be yours."

The deer thought, and said, "I wish that no wild creature in your kingdom be killed."

The king granted this wish and ordered that all wild creatures be protected in his kingdom. Thus the wisdom of the golden deer brought about a time of peace and plenty.

# The Viper
# and the Monk

ONG AGO, in one of the many beautiful valleys of the Himalayan foothills, there lived a group of young monks who were being trained by a senior monk.

One day, a baby viper found its way into the hut of one of the young monks. The monk took an immediate liking to the little snake and decided to keep him as his pet. He made a home for the viper in a large, hollow piece of bamboo, which he could close up when he wished. The other young monks thought this was rather strange behavior. They began calling the viper Bamboo. They called the young monk Bamboo's father.

When the senior monk heard of this, he called Bamboo's father to see him.

"Is it true that you are keeping a viper as a pet?" asked the teacher.

"Yes," said the young monk. "I love him dearly."

"Wild creatures belong in the wild. A viper can never be trusted," said the senior monk. "If you keep him, you could well bring death upon yourself."

"I love him as a teacher loves his students," pleaded Bamboo's father. "I could not live without him."

The young monk returned to his hut, and the weeks passed. One day, a group of young monks set out to gather fruit, and Bamboo's father was among them. He placed Bamboo in his cage before he left and assured the snake he would be back soon. The fruit, however, was hard to find, and the monks had to walk very far in their search. Three days passed before they returned. When the young monk at last entered his hut he remembered that poor Bamboo had not been fed in all the time he had been gone. He felt sorry that he had been so neglectful. He took a piece of fruit and, opening the bamboo cage, said, "You must be so hungry, Bamboo. Come and

eat." Bamboo was crazed with hunger, and instead of taking the fruit, he struck out and bit the young monk's hand. Bamboo's father collapsed, dead. Bamboo escaped into the forest.

As the other young monks were cremating the body of their fallen brother, the senior monk said, with great sadness, "If he had listened to my kind advice, he would not be gone now. To be head-strong can lead to grave results."

# The Black-Maned Lion
# and the Tree

**L**ONG AGO, in a forest bordering the Ganges River, a black-maned lion slept at the foot of a great old babul tree. The wind came and broke a dead branch, which fell on the lion's shoulder. The lion leapt to his feet and looked around for who struck him. He realized that a branch had fallen from the tree. He was a foul-tempered lion, and he became furious with the tree. "How dare you strike me!" he roared. "I am the lord of this forest! You cannot expect to commit such a crime and not be punished!"

But the lion could not think of how he could punish the tree. As if by fate, he saw a group of carpenters walking through the forest with axes and saws.

"Oh, I see how vengeance can be mine," thought the lion. He approached the carpenters meekly so they would not be frightened.

"Hello, my good friends," he called to the men. "It is a fine day for gathering wood for your trade. What do you seek?"

The carpenters were surprised by the lion, but he seemed quite friendly. "We are seeking just the right tree for making the wheels of a cart," they said.

"Oh my!" said the lion. "You are in luck. I know just the tree!" And with that he guided them to the tree under which he had slept.

"You are right!" said the carpenters. "The babul tree is famous for the quality of its wood." So they began chopping down the tree, and the lion lay near them, delighted to watch.

While the men were busy chopping, one of them began to imagine what a fine price the cart would fetch if its seat were covered with the soft skin of a black-maned lion. With a simple twist of his torso he brought his axe down on the neck of the lion.

The tree was felled and the lion was skinned. The lion's vengeful nature led to his own end and that of the great tree as well.

# The Frog and
# the Snake

**L**ONG AGO, along the Ganges River, people set out wicker cages to catch fish. A water snake preyed on the fish in the traps, snatching them from the cages and eating them one by one. One day, he became greedy and swam all the way into a trap, but there were many fish there and they turned on him and bit him from head to tail. Fearing for his life, he fought his way out of the trap and narrowly escaped.

Exhausted and bloodied, he made his way to the edge of the river and rested on some rocks. As he was lamenting his experience, a green frog came hopping along the rocks. "Frog," said the snake, "you would never believe what just happened to me," and he related the episode of the fish in the trap. "Does that seem right to you, good frog?"

"Well, yes, it does seem right, Snake," said the frog. "You eat the fish when they are at your mercy. Why should they not eat you when you are at theirs? The weak are not weak when they are great in number. The biter can well be bitten."

# The Monkey and the Pearl Necklace

 **L**ONG AGO, in Agra, a young prince had a beautiful palace, on the grounds of which was a lovely swimming pond. One hot day the prince and his young bride and her attendants decided to swim to cool off.

The swimmers took off their clothes, folded them, and entered the cool, soothing water. The princess also removed her pearl necklace and placed it on top of her clothes before slipping into the pond.

A monkey had been watching all of this with great interest. From her perch in a tree, her eyes caught sight of the pearl necklace. It glimmered in the light of the sun as nothing she had ever seen. With great stealth, she scurried down the tree, snatched the necklace, and returned to her perch without being seen. She hid the string of pearls in the leaves of the tree.

After a long, enjoyable swim, the royal party came out of the pond and began to dress.

"My necklace is gone!" the princess shrieked.

The prince was furious. "We will find this thief!" he said.

The first to be accused was a gardener who was working nearby. He denied that he had taken the necklace and instead accused the prince's treasurer. But the prince's treasurer denied it and accused the prince's priest. He denied it and accused the prince's chief musician. He denied it and accused his girlfriend. She denied it as well. All were searched, and the necklace was not found.

One of the prince's advisers happened to be watching a group of monkeys at play in the palace garden. He thought, "Monkeys are nearly as notorious as crows for being petty thieves. I wonder if one of them ran off with the necklace while the princess was swimming."

He sent the guards into the gardens to carefully watch the monkeys, and after a few days, sure enough, one of the guards saw the guilty monkey high in the trees. She was wearing the necklace. But how to get the pearls away from her? The adviser had an idea.

He ordered many necklaces made of worthless, shiny beads, and he laid them beneath the tree where the monkey thief was seen. The other monkeys saw the beads and began collecting them. The thief became envious and wanted more necklaces for herself. When she descended, she was caught, and the pearls were recovered. While many of her friends sported shiny necklaces, she now had none.

The princess was delighted to have pearls back and delighted with the adviser who had used his wits to retrieve them.

"It takes more than accusations to find what is missing," she said. "Sometimes you need close observation and cleverness."